MW00948860

Charleigh,
Go explore this great big
world & write about
your adventures!
Love,
Kathryn
Egly

Climb, Soar, Swim, Explore!

Kathryn Egly

Written by Kathryn Egly

Illustrated by Cedric Taylor

Designed by Kristall Willis

Dedicated to my husband, Ted Egly

He's the one who said, "You should write a book!" and
then encouraged me the entire way from idea to publication.

Meet the Magnificent Four Who Love to Explore

From left to right: Luke, Paul, Clark, and George

Early one morning George opened his eyes and could smell the scent of bacon and chocolate chip cookies coming from the kitchen.

"Wow, today must be a special day!" Then he remembered it was the **FIRST** day of **SUMMER VACATION!**

"WOOHOO!" He shouted as he ran down the stairs.

"What should we do today?" He asked his three brothers: Clark, Paul, and Luke.

They all agreed that they wanted to go on an **ADVENTURE.**

"Let's climb Pike's Peak!" George said excitedly.

"We've been studying the animals that live in our region, so let's see how many of them we can find as we hike."

The boys packed their lunch bags with sandwiches, fruit, and warm chocolate chip cookies. They put on their hiking boots and headed out the door.

As they approached the base of the mountain, Clark spotted a rattlesnake.

"Stay back boys!" warned Clark. **"This is a prairie rattlesnake."**

"This type of
snake doesn't
usually attack
people, but it
will strike if
you get too
close. Let's keep
walking and
give that snake
some space.
We've got a lot
more to see."

As the boys went further up the mountain, they spotted a herd of deer. The deer were eating leaves and grass but kept their eyes on the boys.

Paul noticed the deer had their white tails raised. He reminded his brothers deer do this when they are on alert. A raised tail signals to the other deer there is a chance of danger. The boys smiled, waved, and kept on walking to let the deer eat in peace.

Soon they approached a bubbly stream.

"Look, there's a trout!" said Luke.

"Have you ever tried to count their spots?
There are so many! When we get home,
we need to ask Dad to take us fishing.
I love catching and eating trout!
Eagles and hawks love trout too."

10

They got a drink from the cool, clear stream and watched in awe as a beautiful bald eagle swooped down and caught a trout with his sharp claws.

Paul wondered if the eagle was going to feed her eaglets with that trout.

They decided to continue their climb when suddenly there was a loud, thunderous noise in the woods.

"CRACK!!!"

"Did you hear that loud crash?" Paul asked.

"CRACK! CRUNCH!"

"There it was again!" said Paul excitedly.

The boys turned their heads and saw two bighorn sheep had rammed their horns into each other.

"If we bumped our heads like those bighorn sheep do, we'd have a headache!" Paul said.

"That's true!" agreed George. "But bighorn sheep have an extra layer on their head, so they don't feel bumps the same way we do."

The boys finally reached the summit of Pike's Peak and saw a marmot soaking in the sun on top of a rock. Another marmot stood close by, standing guard.

"Marmots stay together in groups called colonies," explained Clark.

"When one marmot is resting or eating, another stands guard to watch out for predators."

The boys sat down to eat the lunch they had packed that morning. They noticed the marmot's nose twitch as he got a scent of those delicious chocolate chip cookies.

"We can never feed the wildlife," George instructed.

"Human food is not healthy for them, and it's not safe for us to feed them."

By this time, the boys were ready to head home.

George heard the bell ring from the Cog Railroad, signaling that it would be descending the mountain.

The boys jumped on board.

George, Clark, Paul, and Luke enjoyed the incredible view from the train on the way down the mountain.

They waved to each of the animals they saw on the way down.

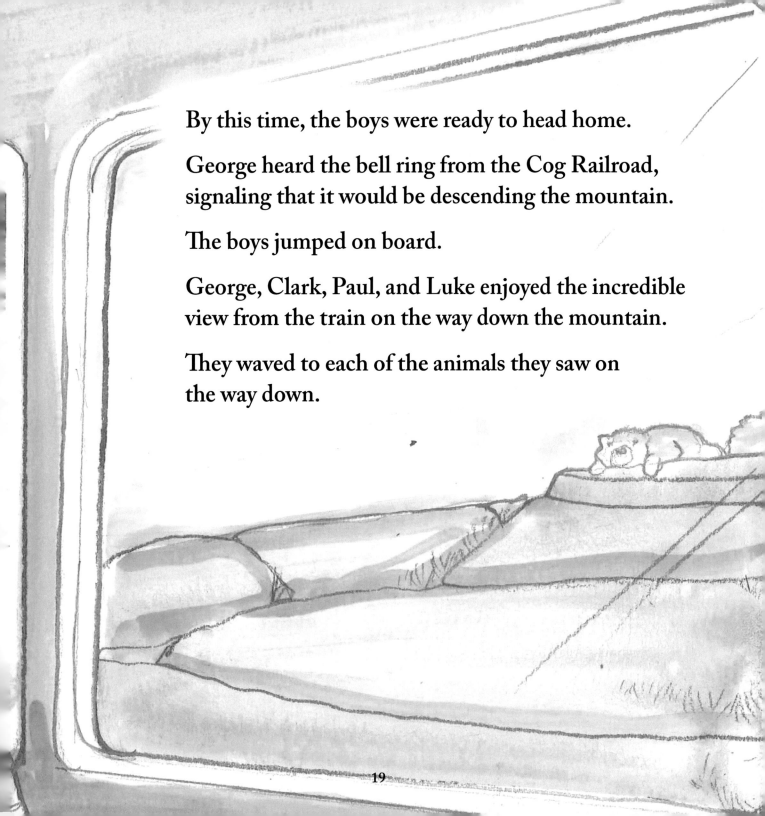

The boys arrived home and told Mom and Dad all about their day of adventure and about each of the animals they had discovered on Pike's Peak.

While they slept that night, they dreamed about the other adventures they wanted to take during their summer vacation.

George dreamed of exploring the caves in Colorado.

Clark dreamed of playing football with the Denver Broncos and winning the Super Bowl.

Paul dreamed of biking across Colorado!

Luke dreamed of discovering a mystery creature in the Garden of the Gods.

The End

About the Author

Kathryn Egly is "Mom" to the Magnificent Four (also known as the "Cowboys"). She loves good books, hot coffee, and her handsome husband. They've called Colorado "home" since 2015 and enjoy discovering the endless beauty all around them. You can follow their adventures on her blog at kathrynegly.com!

Illustrator: Cedric Taylor (cedrictaylorgraphics@gmail.com)

Graphic Designer: Kristall Willis (kwdesignsco.com . kwdesignsco@gmail.com)

Special Thanks

TO THE FOLLOWING SPONSERS FOR HELPING UNDERWRITE THIS BOOK:

Alma and Ned Freeman - Great Grandparents of the Magnificent Four

Dave Freeman aka "Poppy" - In memory of my special friend, Challie.
  The little dog rescued from the Dallas Airport and named for the
  Challenger jet that carried her home on that day.
  She would love exploring Pike's Peak!

Chris and Rebecca Bornman - Grandparents

Mason, Katelynn, Jack and Lily Shoemaker - Cousins

Brent and Karen Freeman and family - Great Uncle, Aunt and Cousins.

Donna Cupailo of Port Jefferson, NY

Daniel and Susan Blevins - In honor of their dog, Lacy

Made in the USA
Lexington, KY
27 December 2017